A BARBIE DRESS AND READ BOOK

Dancing the Night Away

Stephanie St Pierre

ILLUSTRATIONS BY PRIMARY DESIGN

FANTAIL

FANTAIL BOOKS

Published by the Penguin Group
Penguin Books Ltd, 27 Wrights Lane, London W8 5TZ, England
Penguin Books USA Inc., 375 Hudson Street, New York, New York 10014, USA
Penguin Books Australia Ltd, Ringwood, Victoria, Australia
Penguin Books Canada Ltd, 10 Alcorn Avenue, Toronto, Ontario, Canada M4V 3B2
Penguin Books (NZ) Ltd, 182–190 Wairau Road, Auckland 10, New Zealand

Penguin Books Ltd, Registered Offices: Harmondsworth, Middlesex, England

First published in the USA by Price Stern Sloan 1991
Published by Fantail Books 1992
10 9 8 7 6 5 4 3

Printed in England by Clays Ltd, St Ives plc
Filmset in Monophoto Baskerville

Contents

For Cheryl Babb
with many thanks

Introduction

Barbie's life is full of glamour and excitement. Now you can join her in that fabulous world as you read this story.

Fashion and clothes have always been very important to Barbie and as you read this adventure you will notice descriptions of her outfits.

You might like to dress your Barbie in the same clothes or maybe find another outfit which you think will suit the occasion. Use your imagination to create a look that you think works the best.

Enjoy reading the story and have fun dressing your Barbie at the same time.

1

Getting Ready

"Barbie! Barbie, where are you?" called a voice from under a table.

"I'm right here, Christie," Barbie answered. "What are you doing down there?"

"I'm looking for a place to plug in these lights." Christie held up a string of tiny white bulbs. Barbie had got a small group of friends together to decorate the Community Hall for a Dance Marathon. The Dance-a-thon would help to raise money for Children's Charities, a group that helped poor children.

Christie worked as a fund-raiser for Children's Charities. When they decided to have a Dance Marathon, Christie knew that Barbie was the perfect person to put in charge.

Barbie found lots of bands to come and play at the Dance-a-thon. She picked the food for people to eat. She had ideas for the decorations. And when people heard that Barbie would be performing too, everyone in town wanted to come and dance the night away. The money people paid for their tickets would help to open a new day-care centre.

"I don't think I'm very good at setting up lights," said Christie. She came out from under the table. "What else can I do?"

"Let's see," Barbie said. She looked at the list she was carrying. "Maybe we should do the mirrors." The girls had decided to decorate with mirrors and lights and silver streamers.

"What time is Midge coming to practise?" asked Christie. She and Midge and Barbie had their own rock and roll band, Barbie and the Beat. They would be performing at the Dance-a-thon.

"She should be here at six o'clock," said Barbie. "When she's finished work."

"Maybe Steven and Ken can do the lights," said Christie. "I'll find them."

"Great," said Barbie. "They can help with the stage lights too." While Christie was gone, Barbie ticked things off her list. There were still an awful lot of jobs to do, and only three days left before the Dance-a-thon!

"OK," Christie said. "I found them."

"Hi," said Ken.

"What can we do to help?" asked Steven.

"Our goal today," said Barbie, "is to get all the lights strung, and hang mirrors and streamers. You guys do the lights."

"OK," said Ken. He and Steven set to work. Barbie and Christie chose places to hang the mirrors. Skipper and her friend Courtney suddenly appeared.

"Can we help?" they asked.

"You can put the silver tablecloths on all the tables," said Barbie. Skipper and Courtney ran off giggling to do their job.

"Now let's hammer in the hooks for the mirrors," Barbie said.

"I'm glad you're so organized," said Christie. "I don't think I could keep track of everything."

"Neither could I if I lost this list," Barbie said. She put it down on a table and got two hammers from the tool-box.

"If it weren't for all the time we lost because of Lynn, we wouldn't be rushing now," said Christie.

"Get some of your anger out with this," said Barbie. She handed Christie a hammer and some hooks and nails.

"Grrr," Christie growled. She hammered a hook into the wall and laughed. "I guess it won't help to be mad."

"No," said Barbie. "Let's just get the work done. Everything will be fine."

4

"Whoever finishes last," said Christie, "buys pizza for everybody."

"It's a deal," said Barbie. "Let's go."

The girls worked quickly. Barbie finished a second before Christie did. "I win!" she cried.

"I'll order the pizza. You tell the gang that food is coming," said Christie.

"Pizza time!" Barbie called. Ken and Steven were at the other end of the long room. Skipper's boyfriend, Kevin, was with them.

"All right!" the guys shouted back.

"Pizza will be here soon," said Christie when she came back. She helped Barbie hang some more mirrors. The last one was in place when the pizza arrived.

"Perfect timing," said Barbie. Everyone took some pizza and a can of fizzy drink.

"This is fun," said Barbie. She was just beginning to think that everything would be ready on Saturday night. Even with the delays that Lynn had caused. But then again . . .

"Excuse me," called a loud angry voice. "*Excuse me*. Is anybody here?"

"Oh, no," groaned Christie. "Not her again."

"Lynn," said Barbie with a sigh.

2

The Missing List

Barbie got up from the floor. A short pretty girl with curly brown hair was standing near the entrance to the hall. "We're over here, Lynn." Lynn quickly shoved something into her pocket. Then she walked towards the others. Her heels clicked noisily across the floor.

"I wanted to know if you'd thought things over," Lynn said.

"You mean about letting you be in charge of the Dance-a-thon?" Barbie asked. Lynn nodded. "The truth is, I wouldn't feel right giving up the job," Barbie said. Lynn was jealous that Barbie had got the job. She had been trying to get Barbie to quit from the start. In fact, she had told Christie not to ask Barbie in the first place.

"I think you're just being selfish," said Lynn. "I've worked for Children's Charities for two years. And my father is their biggest sponsor. And I'm just as good a dancer as you are." She stamped her foot and pouted.

"Christie asked me to take the job and I can't back out," said Barbie. "But there are lots of other things you could do."

"I'm not interested in doing all the hard work while you get all the applause," said Lynn. "If I can't be the star, then why should I do anything?" Lynn shoved her hands deep into her coat pockets. "This is your last chance," she said. "If you won't let me do it, you'll be sorry."

"Lynn, you can't mean that," said Barbie. She felt sorry for Lynn, but she was also getting annoyed. "Remember we're doing this to help the kids who need the day-care centre."

"Oh, you are just impossible!" cried Lynn. Then she left in a huff.

"What's her problem?" asked Steven.

"She's a spoiled brat," said Christie.

"Lynn isn't very happy that Christie asked me to be in charge," said Barbie.

"If she had the job she wouldn't have done half as much work as you have," said Christie. "And she's so snobby."

"Oh, I feel kind of sorry for her," said Barbie. "I don't think she means to be so awful."

"Well," said Christie. "She's going to cause trouble, I'm sure."

"What could she do?" Ken asked.

"Who knows?" said Christie.

"In the meantime," Barbie said, "we've still got a zillion things to do." She threw her drink can into the recycling bin and went to the table near the doors to pick up her papers. "Hey, did anybody see where I left my list?"

"Wasn't it right there?" Christie asked.

"I thought so," said Barbie. "But it's not there now." She looked around. Finally she found it on the floor under the table. "That's strange," she said. She folded the papers up and stuck them in her pocket.

"Does this mean our break is over?" asked Steven.

"No," said Barbie, laughing. "Christie and I have to hang streamers before Midge gets here. But you guys can keep on eating." Ken and Steven smiled and munched pizza happily. Skipper and Courtney had already gone back to doing tablecloths.

"All right," said Christie. "I'm ready." There were shiny silver streamers and sparkly silver fringes to hang from the ceiling, around the mirrors and on the walls. "This is going to be beautiful." She stood on a ladder while Barbie held the bottom.

"I can't wait to see it with the lights," said Barbie.

The girls were about halfway through putting up the decorations when Midge arrived.

"Hi," she called. "I've got our stuff in the car. Let's get it and set it up on the stage."

"Good idea," said Barbie. Barbie, Christie and Midge soon had their microphones set up and their instruments unpacked. Barbie was playing electric guitar. Midge was playing the drums. Christie was playing the electric piano.

"OK, one, two, three . . ." Barbie counted out the beat. "Let's sing!" Music blasted into the big empty room.

"Betcha all like to dance and move," they sang into their microphones. Skipper and Courtney and Kevin were dancing and singing along. Barbie danced around the stage. Halfway through the song Ken and Steven called for Barbie to stop the music.

"You sound fantastic, but you've got

to see this," Steven called. "We've got all the lights up."

Ken turned off the main lights. It was pitch-dark in the room for a minute. Then Steven started turning on the strings of tiny white lights. The room began to glitter. The silver streamers shimmered. The mirrors reflected the light back into the room.

"It's like being inside a giant diamond," cried Barbie. She imagined the room filled with hundreds of dancers. She could hardly wait until Saturday night!

3

A Rotten Trick

Barbie woke up to the sound of her phone ringing. She'd overslept.

"Hello?" she said sleepily.

"Barbie, we've got a problem at the Community Hall." It was Christie. She sounded upset.

"What is it?" Barbie asked, suddenly waking up.

"You'd better get down here right away," said Christie. "All I can tell you is we've got two thousand little sandwiches sitting in the middle of the hall."

"What!?" cried Barbie. "I'll be there as soon as I can." Barbie jumped out of bed and quickly dressed in black leggings and a fluffy pink sweater. She washed her face, ran a brush through her hair and put on a little pink lipstick. Five minutes later she was in the driver's seat of her Ferrari. "How could the food for the Dance-a-thon have arrived two days early?" she wondered.

Christie looked relieved when Barbie came running into the Hall.

"What's going on?" Barbie asked. A man was carrying a big tray full of tiny sandwiches.

"I'm so glad you're here," said Christie. "I didn't know what to do." Another man came in carrying a tray of cheese and crackers and fruit. Barbie stared in disbelief at the tables overflowing with food.

"Excuse me," she said to the first man. "Why is this food being delivered now?"

"My boss called me last night to make sure I could deliver everything today, extra early," he said.

"But we ordered the food for Saturday afternoon!" said Barbie.

"A young lady called and changed the order," said the man. "She told us the food had to be ready and delivered this morning. I'll tell you, it wasn't easy for the cooks to get everything done so quickly."

"Well, I'm really sorry, but there's been a terrible mistake," Barbie began.

"I'm sorry too," said the man. "The food is here, as ordered. It has to be paid for. You should be glad they didn't charge you extra for the rush job."

"But we can't keep it here," said Barbie. "You'll have to take it back until Saturday."

"I can't," said the man. "We don't have that much storage space." As they talked two other men continued to bring in food. There were now four long tables full of food.

"Let me call your boss," she said. "I

16

just don't understand how this could have happened." The man shrugged again and went back to work. Barbie went to the pay phone outside to call the caterer.

"I'm sorry, Barbie," he said. "But a young woman called last night. She said she was helping you with the Dance-a-thon. I thought it was strange, but I had no way of knowing. We worked all night to get everything ready for this morning."

"I'm sorry about that," said Barbie. "I think I've just figured out how this mix-up happened." It must have been Lynn. What a mean, rotten trick!

"I'd take the food back if I could," said the caterer.

"I know," said Barbie. "If we can find a place to keep it I think we can save most of it until Saturday. Can we freeze the sandwiches?"

"Yes," the caterer said. "And keep the cheese and fruit wrapped up on the platters and in the refrigerator. You'll have to take the crackers off the platters and put them in something else so they don't get soggy."

"Thanks," said Barbie. She hung up the phone. They had a lot of work to do. Barbie sighed. Where would they find a freezer big enough to hold two thousand sandwiches? She went back to the Hall.

"What happened?" Christie asked.

"I think Lynn thought this would be a funny trick," said Barbie. "We're stuck with the food. Do you know anybody with a freezer big enough to hold all those sandwiches and cheese?"

"Steven's dad is a butcher. He has a huge freezer and refrigerator at his shop," said Christie.

"Fantastic!" cried Barbie. "Let's see if he can help." Christie called Steven and soon everything was arranged.

"Steven will drop by later to pick up the food," Christie said. "Thank goodness."

"So Lynn's trick didn't spoil anything after all," said Barbie. "Except my plans for the day."

"That girl is too much," said Christie. She shook her head. "What can we do about her?"

"I don't think there's anything to do," said Barbie with a sly smile. "Except let her be in charge."

"No way!" said Christie.

"Well, seriously," said Barbie. "Maybe we could let her do one of the dance numbers. She is a good dancer."

"I don't want to have anything to do with her," said Christie. "But if you think that might help, go ahead."

"It might be worth a try," said Barbie. "Now, do you want to wrap sandwich trays or unwrap cheese and put away the crackers?" Christie just groaned.

4
Fun at the Shopping Centre

Around lunch-time Barbie and Christie finished sorting out the food.

"How about going shopping?" asked Barbie.

"That sounds like fun," said Christie. The girls hopped into Barbie's Ferrari and drove into town. They sang along to a favourite song on the radio. The wind whipped through their hair. It was a terrific day for a ride in a convertible.

"What are you shopping for?" asked Christie.

"I need an outfit for the Latin dance I'm doing," said Barbie. "And the opening number. Ken and I are doing a great routine. First it's ballroom dancing, then it ends with some really pretty ballet."

"How about some new outfits for Barbie and the Beat?" asked Christie. "Our old ones are getting kind of boring."

"OK," said Barbie. "But what about Midge?"

"Let's surprise her," said Christie. "We can go around to her house tonight and try on our new outfits before we practise." By the time they got to the shopping centre, Barbie and Christie had a busy afternoon planned.

"I like this store," said Barbie. They walked through a designer boutique looking at ball gowns. Christie held up a blue-feathered gown with silver sequins.

"Maybe," said Barbie. She held up a hot-pink ruffled gown. It was short at the front and had a long ruffled train at the back. The top was silvery-pink, with more ruffles around the shoulders. "This might work for the Latin dance."

"Oh, here's one that will look great on you," said Christie. She held out a beautiful peach gown. It had a full skirt with lots of layers of shimmery silk. The top had a pretty rose on it and short puffed sleeves.

"It's so elegant," said Barbie. "It would be great for the opening number."

Finally Barbie had picked out enough gowns. She disappeared into the changing-room. Christie waited outside.

"Well, what do you think?" Barbie asked. She came out of the changing-room wearing the blue dress Christie had found.

"It really brings out the colour of your eyes," said Christie.

"But I don't like the feathers," said Barbie. She went back to try on another gown and was out again in a minute.

22

"Wow!" said Christie. "That one is wild." Barbie had on the hot-pink ruffled gown.

"I love the way the skirt moves when I dance." Barbie cha-cha-cha'd across the floor.

"It's really great," agreed Christie.

Barbie danced back to the changing-room. This time she was gone a little longer. When she reappeared she looked wonderfully glamorous. She was wearing the peach gown.

"Oh, it's wonderful," Christie said.

"And the best thing," said Barbie, "is that it's two pieces! The skirt and top are separate." She made a graceful turn. The skirt swept out around her. "This will be just right for the opening number. I can pull off the skirt backstage and slip into a tutu in no time. The top will look wonderful with a peach tutu, won't it?"

"You'll be so beautiful," said Christie.

Barbie went back to the changing-room

and quickly changed into her own clothes. She bought the hot-pink dress and the peach gown. Christie and Barbie walked on looking in different shops. "I want something that will really stand out," said Christie.

"How about this?" Barbie held up a bright fluorescent yellow outfit with a tight skirt and a cropped top with a pink ruffle. The colour looked great against Christie's dark skin.

"I love it," cried Christie. "And look, they have more in different colours." Barbie chose a pink outfit for herself and an orange one for Midge. Then they went to try them on.

"I think they're terrific," said Barbie. "But something is missing."

"I know," said Christie. "Jackets!"

"And boots!" said Barbie. The girls bought the outfits and then spent the rest of their afternoon shopping for accessories. They found long boots with fluorescent piping and denim jackets with ruffles and fringes, studded with sparkly fake gems.

"Won't Midge be surprised?" Barbie said happily. The day had turned out much better than she'd expected.

5

Songs and Surprises

"I love it!" Midge said. She was wearing her new outfit. The neon-orange top and skirt were perfect with her long red hair and freckled face. "I have a great idea," she said. "You guys put on your new outfits and let's all go out for hamburgers."

"Shouldn't we save these outfits for Saturday?" said Christie.

"Oh, come on," said Barbie. "We'll tell everybody who notices our outfits that they're for the Dance-a-thon. It's great advertising."

"Good idea!" said Christie. Barbie and Christie changed. The girls stood together in front of Midge's full-length mirror.

"Very, very cool," said Midge. Christie

and Barbie agreed. "But I think we need some make-up to go with these outfits." She got out a load of lipsticks and eye-shadows to play with.

"Oh, I almost forgot," said Barbie. "I got earrings too." She ran back to the living-room where she'd left the shopping bags. "Here they are," she said. She held out three pairs of fluorescent yellow, pink and orange earrings.

"Wild," said Midge.

"Terrific," said Christie. They put on their earrings and finished their make-up. Another look in the mirror and they knew they looked perfect.

"Let's go," said Barbie. They took a Barbie and the Beat tape with them so they could practise singing some songs in the car.

"I can't wait until Saturday," said Midge. "It's going to be so much fun."

"And everybody is going to be there!" said Christie.

"That's for sure," said Midge. "I'm a little nervous about playing in front of all those radio DJ's and TV people."

"That reminds me," said Barbie. "I need to call the TV station to make sure they come at the right time. We were so busy today, I forgot all about my list of things to do."

"The thing to do now," said Midge, "is sing." She put on the tape.

"If you ever feel afraid of what you cannot see then listen to the rap . . . Listen carefully . . ." The girls sang along. They were still singing when they got to the restaurant. Everyone in the car-park stared. Barbie honked the horn and waved to some friends.

In no time a crowd had gathered around the car. Barbie, Midge and Christie sang until the tape ended. Everyone was clapping and yelling for more.

"Come to the Dance-a-thon on

Saturday night!" Barbie called out to the
crowd. "Barbie and the Beat will be
there." The girls went inside. Many
people followed them, asking questions
about the Dance-a-thon.

"You can get tickets at the Community
Hall," Christie said. "The money goes to
Children's Charities."

"There will be food and great music,"
Barbie said. "And dancing all night
long." Finally the crowd thinned out.

"Well, you were right about these
outfits being good for some advertising,"
said Christie. "Now everyone in town will
know about the dance marathon." Barbie
and Midge laughed. They had made a
pretty big entrance. But the place was
quietening down.

They found a quiet table in a corner.
The girls looked at their menus. Thinking
the waitress had come, Barbie looked up.
It wasn't the waitress at all. It was
trouble.

"Lynn," said Barbie. Lynn Madison smiled sweetly at Barbie.

"How's everything going with your Dance-a-thon?" she asked. She almost started to giggle.

"I don't think what you did was very funny," said Christie.

"What are you talking about?" asked Lynn.

"We know it was you who changed our food order," Christie said. "That was a rotten thing to do. Even for you."

"Oh, are you having trouble with your caterer?" said Lynn. "That's too bad." Lynn's friends were calling her back to her table. "Sorry I can't stay to hear about it," she said. She started to laugh as she walked away.

"We've got to do something about her," said Midge.

"Maybe this would be a good time to offer her that dance number," said

Barbie. She got up and went over to where Lynn was sitting.

"Lynn, I wanted to ask you something," said Barbie.

"Well, what?" asked Lynn.

"We were wondering if you would like to perform at the Dance-a-thon," said Barbie. "Everyone knows you're a terrific dancer. What do you say?"

"Hmm," Lynn thought for a minute. "I'll have to think about it." Barbie knew Lynn wanted to say yes. But her pride got in the way.

"There isn't much time left," said Barbie. "But I can give up one of my spots if you decide you want to perform."

"I'll let you know," said Lynn. She didn't seem to want to fight as much suddenly. Maybe Barbie's plan would work. Maybe if Lynn had something fun to do, she wouldn't cause any more problems. Maybe.

6

So Much to Remember

"What happened?" asked Christie. Three juicy hamburgers sat on the table. A plate of french-fries was in the middle for everyone to share.

"I offered her a dance number," said Barbie. "She said she didn't know if she wanted to do it or not."

"Let's forget about her," said Midge. The girls ate and talked about the Dance-a-thon. They were looking forward to trying out some new songs they had written. They had forgotten all about Lynn when suddenly she was standing at their table again.

"I've decided I'll do it," Lynn said. "I'll dance."

"That's great, Lynn," said Barbie. Christie raised her eyebrows. Midge looked at her plate. "Come to the Community Hall tomorrow, and you can rehearse."

"Fine," said Lynn. "I'll be there." She left without saying good-bye.

"I still don't trust her," said Christie.

"Me neither," said Midge. "I'll bet she's planning something sneaky."

"Come on, you guys," said Barbie. "She just wants to be included. I think she'll be nicer now that she's got something fun to do."

"But what about what happened today?" asked Christie. "Have you forgotten about the food?"

"No," said Barbie. "But I'm hoping that Lynn will feel sorry about causing so much trouble. I think she'll try to make up for it too."

"Well, you're in charge," said Christie. "But I'm going to keep a close watch on her."

When they'd finished dinner they all went home. It had been a long day, but Barbie still had work to do.

"Now where did I leave that list?" she wondered. She found it in one of the pockets of the trousers she'd worn the day before. But something was wrong. "The second page of the list is missing," she said. Barbie checked her trouser pockets again. There was nothing in them. She looked everywhere, but the missing page was nowhere to be found.

"I have to find that list," Barbie cried. She picked up the phone and called Christie.

"Hi," she said. "Did you see a page from my Things do Do list at the Community Hall?"

"No," said Christie. "And if it was left there, it's gone by now. The caretaker was going to wash and wax the floors tonight."

"Oh dear," said Barbie. "I guess I'll

just have to remember what was on that page. I can't believe I lost it."

"Are you sure you *did* lose it?" asked Christie.

"What do you mean?" asked Barbie.

"Well, could Lynn have taken it?"

"Hmm . . ." Barbie thought. "She was acting pretty strange yesterday at the Community Hall. And after she left, I couldn't find my list. It was on the floor by the door she went out of."

"Right," said Christie. "Lynn could have seen the list, ripped out a page and then just dropped it when she saw you coming."

"Maybe I should call her," said Barbie.

"She won't tell you if she took it," said Christie.

"No," said Barbie. "But I might be able to make it easy for her to give it back."

"Good luck," said Christie.

"Thanks," Barbie said. She looked Lynn's number up in the phone book and called her.

"Hi, Lynn. It's Barbie," she said.

"Uh, oh, hi," said Lynn.

"I'm sorry to bother you, but I have a problem I was hoping you could help me with," said Barbie.

"Well, what is it?" asked Lynn.

"I lost an important list I needed for the Dance-a-thon," said Barbie.

"What's that got to do with me?" said Lynn.

"I wondered if you might have seen it," said Barbie. There was a long pause.

"I'm sorry, but I can't help you," said Lynn.

"Too bad," said Barbie. "I guess I'll see you at rehearsal then."

"Yes," said Lynn. "I'll see you then." Barbie was sure that Lynn knew more about the list than she was saying. Maybe she would feel guilty and bring it back tomorrow. Maybe not. Barbie knew she'd have to try to rewrite the list.

"Let's see," Barbie said. "The first thing was to pick up my ballet shoes." Barbie wrote that down. "Then there was flowers for the tables, and I needed to write out the schedule for the bands, and I needed to find a few volunteers to take tickets at the door on Saturday night.

"Was that everything?" Barbie was too tired to remember any more tonight.

7
A Terrible Mistake

The Community Hall was buzzing with people. Barbie and Ken were getting ready to run through their opening dance number. Christie and Steven were fixing up the stage sets for the different dance numbers.

A television crew was testing the lighting and planning where to put their cameras. A DJ was setting up records for Barbie and Ken's dance.

"Hi, big sister," said Skipper. She and Courtney had come to watch the dance rehearsal.

"This place is crazy today," said Barbie. She was wearing a pink leotard and tights with pink-and-white-striped leg warmers. "But I'm really glad you came to watch." Barbie hugged her little sister and then started to do her warm-up exercises.

Soon she and Ken were ready to begin. They got into position and waited for the music to start. They began by dancing in great sweeping circles around the centre of the room. Skipper and her friend clapped.

"Wait until we've finished," called Barbie. They glided and twirled beautifully. Before the end of the number the music changed, and the dance switched from ballroom dancing to ballet. Barbie stood on one toe as Ken held her hand and spun her around. Her long blonde hair flew out around her face as she twirled. Then she did a few pliés and some turns. She and Ken were far apart now. Barbie gracefully spun towards Ken. Finally she took a leap into Ken's arms. He held her up in the air. The music ended. Everyone was clapping.

As the applause died down Barbie noticed Lynn standing at the edge of the crowd. She was frowning. Barbie waved to catch her attention.

"Hi, Lynn," she said. "Come over and tell us what sort of dance number you're planning." Lynn made a face but walked over to Barbie and Ken. The crowd was wandering away.

"That was nice," said Lynn. She didn't seem to like admitting that Barbie and Ken had just given a terrific performance.

"Thanks," said Barbie. "I think we've worked it out pretty well. What are you going to do? And how can we help?"

"I'm doing a jazz piece," said Lynn. "I brought a tape. But I didn't know I'd have to practise in front of an audience." She frowned again at the people scattered around the room.

"If you want to practise alone we can clear most of these people out of here in a while," said Barbie. Lynn was still frowning. She looked angry. "Is something wrong?" Barbie asked.

"Why are you being so nice to me?" Lynn asked.

"I guess that's just me," said Barbie. "We're all working for a good cause here. It would be nice if we could be friends." She wondered if Lynn was feeling guilty about the list, and about messing up the food order.

"Look," said Lynn. "I'm sorry I acted so badly. I'm really glad you asked me to dance. That's the only thing I really cared about anyway." Lynn stalked off to give the DJ her tape.

"She has a funny way of saying she's sorry," said Ken. He put his arm around Barbie's shoulder and gave her a hug. "You're being so patient with her," he said. "But none of us can figure out why."

"She's just embarrassed," said Barbie.

"I don't think she has too many friends. And –" Barbie suddenly noticed Lynn had kicked something under the DJ's table. It looked like a piece of paper squashed into a ball. It must be the missing page of her list! She walked slowly towards the table. She was almost there. Then Skipper was ahead of her.

"Hey," called Skipper. "You dropped something." She picked up the paper and took it to Lynn.

"Um, that's not mine," said Lynn.

"But I saw it fall," said Skipper. "Maybe you didn't know it dropped."

"It isn't mine," Lynn said. She sounded angry now. Poor Skipper was only trying to be helpful.

"I think it's mine," said Barbie. She reached for the paper.

"But . . ." Skipper began. She looked from Barbie to Lynn. She could tell that something was very wrong. Lynn grabbed the paper suddenly. Skipper decided to let Barbie and Lynn work things out alone.

"So, you caught me," said Lynn.

"Let's just forget the whole thing," said Barbie. "Give me the list and it's over."

"You were tricking me to get me to bring back that stupid list," said Lynn. "You never meant for me to do a dance number!"

"No, Lynn," said Barbie. "I asked you to do the dance number because I thought you'd do a good job."

"I don't believe you," cried Lynn. "Here's what I think of your important list!" She tore the paper into tiny shreds and threw it in the air. "I'm not staying around here just to be laughed at." Lynn turned and ran.

"Wait!" Barbie called. Everyone was staring now. "Come back!" Lynn kept running.

8

Working It Out

Barbie hurried after Lynn. Lynn had almost reached her car when Barbie came out of the Community Hall.

"Please wait," Barbie called. She started to run down the steps to the carpark but tripped and twisted her ankle. "Ouch!" Barbie cried. She sat down on the steps and rubbed her hurt ankle. It was very sore. Barbie watched as Lynn's little red sports car disappeared into the traffic.

"Barbie, what happened?" It was Ken. He ran down the steps. "Are you hurt?"

"I'm afraid so," said Barbie. "I think I might have sprained my ankle. And all for nothing. I didn't even catch Lynn."

"Let me help you inside," said Ken. "Maybe if you keep ice on it, your ankle will be all right." Ken helped Barbie hop up the steps and inside.

"What happened?" cried Midge and Christie. They ran to their friend. Ken got a chair for Barbie to sit on and another one for her to rest her foot on. Christie found some ice and wrapped it in a scarf. Barbie held it on her sore ankle.

"Lynn must be happy now," said Christie. "I can't believe she didn't help you back inside."

"No," said Barbie. "She's not happy at all. And I don't think she knows I got hurt. I don't think she even heard me calling." Barbie remembered the hurt look on Lynn's face as she ran away.

"What was she so upset about?" asked Midge. "Why did she run away?"

"She was trying to return the list that she had taken," said Barbie. "She was

trying to patch things up. I think she
really wanted a chance to dance for a big
audience. She was scared. So she acted
tough."

"She didn't have to play those mean
tricks on us," said Christie.

"I know," said Barbie. "Still, she
wanted to make things better. And then
. . . she thought we were trying to make
fun of her," said Barbie. "That's why she
ran away."

"But what about you?" asked Christie.
"Are you going to be able to dance
tomorrow?"

Christie looked very upset. She was
worried about her friend. She was also
worried that if people knew Barbie was
hurt, they might not come to the Dance-
a-thon. If no one came, they wouldn't
make enough money to open the day-care
centre.

"I think I'll be able to dance when I
have to," said Barbie. "But I'm not going

to be dancing the night away just for fun."

"Is there anything we can do for you?" asked Midge.

"Yes," said Barbie. "It's too bad Lynn tore up that list. I keep thinking there was something important on it that I've forgotten. Anyway . . ." Barbie made up a list of things for Christie to do. Then she made one for Midge. "I can sit at home and make phone calls," said Barbie. "But you'll have to do the things that call for walking and standing and running around." She laughed. Midge laughed too. Christie managed a small smile.

"Oh, how could this happen?" said Christie.

"Don't worry," said Barbie. "I'll be fine. And I'll still do a great job for you." Barbie was disappointed that she wouldn't be able to do much dancing at the Dance-a-thon. But she knew that her ankle would be OK for the important

dance numbers she had planned to do –
if she was careful. Still, she was worried
about Lynn.

"I know you'll do a good job. You
always do," said Christie. "I'm just sorry
that you got hurt."

"Well, if you think you can take care
of things here," said Barbie, "I'll go home
now." Christie and Midge promised to
take charge. Skipper got her sister's dance
bag. Then Ken helped Barbie to her car
and drove Skipper and Barbie home.

Later that night Midge stopped by to
see Barbie.

"There really isn't all that much more
to do," said Midge. "Everything went
fine."

"I'm really glad we got the decorations
up early," Barbie said.

"How's the ankle?" asked Midge.

"It's OK," said Barbie. "A little sore
though. The only think I don't think I'll
be able to do is that Latin dance number.

I'd rather do the opening act and a good closing act."

"Then what happens during the empty time?" asked Midge.

"That would be a good time for Lynn to dance," said Barbie.

"If she would do it," said Midge. "Is it worth the effort to get her to come back?"

"I'm not sure," said Barbie. "But this Dance-a-thon is supposed to be about helping people. And that includes Lynn."

"How does Lynn need our help?" asked Midge.

"She's snobby and bullies people because she's scared and jealous all the time," Barbie said. "I think if she felt that she had a few real friends, then she'd be a lot nicer."

"So we have to be her friends, too?" Midge said, frowning.

"Not exactly," said Barbie with a laugh. "But I think if we gave her a dance number she'd feel better about herself and act nicer. Then maybe we'd like her a little better."

"OK," said Midge. "That makes sense to me."

"Let's hope it makes sense to Lynn," said Barbie.

9

Real Friends

Saturday was a very frustrating day for
Barbie. She knew there was something she
had forgotten to do, but she couldn't
remember what it was. She wanted to go
to the Community Hall and keep an eye
on things. But she had to rest her ankle
as much as she could. Barbie put a tape
in the stereo and sang along. Suddenly
there was a knock at the door.

"Who could that be?" Barbie
wondered. It was Lynn! "Where have
you been?" Barbie asked.

"I got your phone messages," Lynn
said. "I needed some time to think. I
guess I was being pretty stupid."

"I think things got kind of confused,"

Barbie said. "Do you want to dance or not?"

"Yes," said Lynn. "I do. But I haven't got a costume, or a stage set, or anything."

"Hmm," said Barbie. "You're a little shorter than I am, but I think we're the same size." She hopped to her bedroom and came back with the hot-pink ruffled dress.

"You'll let me borrow this great dress?" Lynn was amazed. "Why?"

"Because I want every number we do tonight to be perfect," said Barbie. "I was going to wear it for a salsa number. You can use the set for that and this dress."

"What a great idea," said Lynn. "My jazz routine will fit perfectly with the Latin theme."

"I'm glad," said Barbie.

"But I feel so bad about you getting hurt," said Lynn. "I'm sorry. I didn't know my temper could get so out of control."

"It's OK," said Barbie. "Everything will work out. And it's not your fault about my ankle. It just happened."

"If we were friends I'd say you were the best one I ever had," said Lynn.

"Then let's be friends," said Barbie. She smiled at Lynn. Lynn smiled back.

Just then the phone rang.

"Hello," said Barbie. She listened for a minute. "I'll be right over." She hung up the phone and turned to Lynn. "That was Loman's Jewellers. I forgot all about the trophies and the prizes for the Dance Contest!" Barbie was upset. Now instead of calmly getting ready for her big opening dance number for the Dance-a-thon she was going to have to drive into town to pick up the forgotten prizes.

"Wait," said Lynn. "Let me go. I don't have to perform until much later. I can pick the things up and bring them to the

Dance-a-thon. I'll still have time to go home and practise a little and change."

"That's fantastic," said Barbie.

"Are you sure you trust me?" Lynn asked.

"Yes, I do," said Barbie. "Friend." Barbie handed Lynn the hot-pink dress.

"See you at the Community Hall," said Lynn. She left with a happy smile on her face. Barbie felt good too. She looked at her watch. There was plenty of time to get ready.

So the two things she had worried about were worries no more. Lynn was happy and Barbie had taken care of everything, even though there had been a lot of unexpected problems. And very little time for mistakes. Thank goodness the jewellers had called. It would have been terrible if there hadn't been any prizes or trophies for the winners of the dance contests.

Barbie took a long bubble bath and

then washed her hair. While it was
drying, she put on her make-up. She wore
pink blusher, blue eye-liner and bright
pink lipstick. She twisted her hair up into
a curly ponytail. With all her costume
changes, she needed a simple hairdo.
She would put a different pretty clip or
ribbon in her hair for each costume.
She wrapped a pale-peach ribbon, with
a big ivory rose, around her ponytail.
That would match her gown for the first
number.

"Now, I'd better get dressed," she said.
She put on the top of her gown and her
peach-coloured tights. She pulled a pair
of leggings on over them. She would wait
until she got to the Hall before she put
on her full skirt so it wouldn't get
crushed.

'I guess that's everything," she said,
putting her make-up case into the bag
with all of her gowns and costumes. The
doorbell rang.

"Christie and Midge, right on time," she said. Her friends were dressed in their Barbie and the Beat outfits.

"This is so exciting," said Midge.

"It's going to be a fantastic night," said Christie.

"I think you're right," agreed Barbie.

10
Dance Magic

"Hello, everybody!" Barbie stood alone on-stage. She was wearing her beautiful, sparkling peach gown. All around her the huge dark room glittered with tiny lights. Hundreds of people watched from the dance floor. A single spotlight shone on Barbie. "Welcome to the Children's Charities Day-care Dance-a-thon."

Everyone cheered and clapped. "Hurrah for Barbie," they cheered. "We love you, Barbie!"

"Thank you all so much for coming tonight," Barbie said. "It's going to be exciting. Is everybody ready to dance the night away?"

The crowd went wild. "Yeah!!!" they shouted.

"Good," Barbie said. "Then I'm going to get you started. Music, please . . ." The music slowly got louder. As it did the stage lit up to reveal a set that looked like a fancy ballroom. Barbie disappeared off-stage for a moment. Then she and Ken came swirling back out. The lights made Barbie's hair shine like gold. Her beautiful smile sparkled. Her blue eyes twinkled. This wasn't just dancing, this was magic!

Finally the music began to slow, and Barbie twirled off-stage again. Ken stood in the lights, waiting. Suddenly Barbie came spinning into the lights again. Now she wore a tutu. The ballet was lovely. When Barbie made her final leap, the crowd was thrilled. "You were great, Barbie," Ken whispered to her. He was worried about her ankle. But she had danced perfectly. The lights blacked out

for a moment. When they came back on, Barbie and Ken stood at the edge of the stage ready to take their bows. Someone handed Barbie a huge bouquet of peach-coloured roses tied with a silk ribbon. When the applause began to fade, Barbie and Ken ran off-stage.

"You were terrific," cried Christie. She gave Barbie a big hug.

"Incredible," said Midge. She hugged Barbie too. Barbie was smiling and laughing.

"It was fun!" she said. "But I need a chair." Someone quickly gave her a seat. She rubbed her sore ankle. "I don't think I'm going to be able to dance with Barbie and the Beat," she said. "I'll need a stool to sit on."

"But we really need somebody dancing," said Christie.

"I have a suggestion," said Barbie. "But I'm not sure if you'll like it."

"Lynn?" guessed Midge.

Barbie nodded.

Christie looked at Barbie and Midge. "OK," she said. "I guess she's proved herself by now."

"We can give her a tambourine," said Barbie. "And don't worry. I'm not going to suggest we make her a member of the band. But for tonight, this will work out fine." Christie left to find Lynn. After Barbie had rested for a little while, she went to change into her outfit for Barbie and the Beat. They wouldn't be playing for a couple of hours, but it was a good outfit to wear hanging around the dance floor.

Barbie was looking forward to walking through the crowd and watching people dance. It was nice to see how much fun they were having. She also wanted to taste those sandwiches.

"Barbie?" called a voice. A tall Asian girl with waist-length black hair was calling her. She was dressed in an acid-green tie-dyed mini-dress with long purple boots. There was a camera hanging from a strap around her neck.

"Kira!" cried Barbie. "What a surprise. I'm so glad to see you." Kira was a friend of Barbie's. They had not seen each other for a long time.

"I'm glad to see you, too," Kira said. "I need to talk to you about something important."

"Let's go outside," said Barbie. They pushed through the jumble of dancers. The music was very loud. Finally they reached the doors.

"That's better," said Kira. They stood on the steps in front of the Community Hall.

"How are you?" asked Barbie.

"I'm fine," said Kira. "I came to town to see if you would like to work on a new project with me."

"Hmm," said Barbie. "What's this one about?" Kira was a photographer. She was always travelling and doing interesting things.

"I'm going to Africa," said Kira. "I'm working with a group that wants to help the wild animals there."

"And where do I fit in?" Barbie wondered.

"We want to make a calendar to sell," said Kira. "But we need a model to be in the photographs with the animals. I thought of you right away."

"Wow," said Barbie. "I think it sounds terrific. I love animals. And I've always wanted to travel in Africa!"

"Hurrah!" said Kira. "Barbie, you're the best!"